SWEETIES

MathStart® ADDITION STRATEGIES

Mall Mania

by Stuart J. Murphy • illustrated by Renée Andriani

HarperCollinsPublishers

To Christopher Mathew, a great addition
to the Murphy clan
—S.J.M.

For Maggie, my mall shopper extraordinaire
—R.A.

The publisher and author would like to thank teachers Patricia Chase, Phyllis Goldman, and Patrick Hopfensperger for their help in making the math in MathStart just right for kids.

HarperCollins®, ®, and MathStart® are registered trademarks of HarperCollins Publishers.
For more information about the MathStart series, write to
HarperCollins Children's Books, 1350 Avenue of the Americas, New York, NY 10019,
or visit our website at www.mathstartbooks.com.

Bugs incorporated in the MathStart series design were painted by Jon Buller.

Library of Congress Cataloging-in-Publication Data
Murphy, Stuart J.
Mall mania / by Stuart J. Murphy ; illustrated by Renée Andriani.— 1st ed.
p. cm. — (MathStart)
"Level 2."
ISBN-10: 0-06-055777-X (pbk.) — ISBN-10: 0-06-055776-1
ISBN-13: 978-0-06-055777-5 (pbk.) — ISBN-13: 978-0-06-055776-8
1. Addition—Juvenile literature. 2. Counting—Juvenile literature. 3. Shopping malls—Juvenile literature. I. Andriani, Renée, ill. II. Title. III. Series.
QA115.M8718 2006 2005002664
513.2'11—dc22 CIP
AC

Typography by Elynn Cohen 1 2 3 4 5 6 7 8 9 10 ❖ First Edition

Be sure to look for all of these **MathStart** books:

LEVEL 1

Beep Beep, Vroom Vroom!
PATTERNS

The Best Bug Parade
COMPARING SIZES

Double the Ducks
DOUBLING NUMBERS

The Greatest Gymnast of All
OPPOSITES

A House for Birdie
UNDERSTANDING CAPACITY

It's About Time!
HOURS

Jack the Builder
COUNTING ON

Leaping Lizards
COUNTING BY 5s AND 10s

Mighty Maddie
COMPARING WEIGHTS

Missing Mittens
ODD AND EVEN NUMBERS

Monster Musical Chairs
SUBTRACTING ONE

One...Two...Three...Sassafras!
NUMBER ORDER

A Pair of Socks
MATCHING

3 Little Fire Fighters
SORTING

LEVEL 2

Bigger, Better, Best!
AREA

Coyotes All Around
ROUNDING

Get Up and Go!
TIME LINES

Give Me Half!
UNDERSTANDING HALVES

Mall Mania
ADDITION STRATEGIES

More or Less
COMPARING NUMBERS

100 Days of Cool
NUMBERS 1-100

Pepper's Journal
CALENDARS

Probably Pistachio
PROBABILITY

Same Old Horse
MAKING PREDICTIONS

Spunky Monkeys on Parade
COUNTING BY 2s, 3s, AND 4s

The Sundae Scoop
COMBINATIONS

Super Sand Castle Saturday
MEASURING

Tally O'Malley
TALLYING

LE

Be
ESTIMATING

Dinosaur Deals
EQUIVALENT VALUES

Divide and Ride
DIVIDING

Earth Day—Hooray!
PLACE VALUE

The Grizzly Gazette
PERCENTAGE

Hamster Champs
ANGLES

Lemonade for Sale
BAR GRAPHS

Less Than Zero
NEGATIVE NUMBERS

Polly's Pen Pal
METRICS

Rodeo Time
READING A SCHEDULE

Safari Park
FINDING UNKNOWNS

Shark Swimathon
SUBTRACTING TWO-DIGIT NUMBERS

Sluggers' Car Wash
DOLLARS AND CENTS

Treasure Map
MAPPING

On Mall Mania Day, the 100th person to enter Parkside Mall would get lots of gifts. The chess club from Wilson Elementary was there to do the counting.

Jonathan, Nicole, Gabby, and Steven stayed at the entrances to count shoppers. Heather, the club captain, and Mr. Grant, the advisor, waited in the food court to give out the prizes. They all had walkie-talkies.

The first people Jonathan saw were his friend Brandon and Brandon's sister, Brooke. "Bye, Brandon. See you later!" said Brooke, as she ran into the mall.

“That’s one,” counted Jonathan.

Brandon stayed outside with Jonathan. “I hate shopping,” he groaned. “But we have to buy a birthday present for our mom. Brooke’s going to find something and then come and get me.”

"Sonny's Sports has just donated two football tickets for the winner!" Mr. Grant announced.

"I hate football," grumbled Brandon. "It's not as good as basketball."

“Listen up!” said Heather. “How many shoppers have come into the mall so far?”

Nicole

Steven

Gabby

Jonathan

Hmm . . . not quite right for Mom. But it looks great on me!

"Nicole and Gabby, add that up," ordered Heather.

"I get 16!" said Nicole.
"Me, too," said Gabby.

“A slow start,” said Heather.

“It’ll pick up,” said Mr. Grant. Then he announced, “The Seafood Shack just donated a free fish dinner.”

“Fish? Yuck!” complained Brandon over the walkie-talkie.

Heather let about ten minutes go by. “Okay,” she said. “How many more people have come in since the last count?”

Nicole

Steven

Gabby

Jonathan

No, this isn't Mom's style. But it just matches my eyes.

"Jonathan and Steven, you do the total," directed Heather.

"The total is 30," said Jonathan.
"That's what I got, too," said Steven.

Heather took out her calculator. "With the 16 we had, that's 46," she said. "Close to halfway!"

"All Ears just donated the latest CD by A-to-Z!" Mr. Grant announced.

"Gross," muttered Brandon. "I never listen to their music."

Pretty soon Heather said, "Count time."

I've got 8.
Nicole
7 here.
Steven
9 at north entrance.
Gabby
8.
Jonathan

Nothing here for Mom—but this looks great with my new shirt.

"Steven and Gabby, what's the total?" asked Heather.

"I get 32!" said Steven.
"Me, too," said Gabby.

“Added to the 46 we had, we’re at 78,” Heather said.
“And the Tee-Shirt Factory has just thrown in a yellow shirt,” Mr. Grant added.

"Yellow's my least favorite color," groaned Brandon.

"Don't you like anything?" asked Jonathan.

"Well, maybe chocolate," said Brandon.

Heather asked for a new count just a few minutes later.

5!
Nicole
5!
Gabby
5!
Steven
6!
Jonathan
What are we going to get for Mom?

"This could be it!" said Heather. "Jonathan and Nicole, what does that add up to?"

"It's 21!" Jonathan and Nicole said eagerly.

"So 21 plus 78 means that we now have a total of 99," exclaimed Heather. "The next person to enter the mall will be our winner!"

Just then, Brooke appeared at the south entrance. "C'mon, Brandon," she called. "I can't find anything for Mom. You've got to help." She grabbed his arm and pulled him into the mall.

"There he is," yelled Jonathan. "The 100th shopper!"

Soon Brandon was standing next to Heather and Mr. Grant in the food court with his prizes: football tickets, a gift certificate for a fish dinner, an A-to-Z CD, and a bright yellow T-shirt. He couldn't believe his bad luck.

100

"And here's one more prize donated at the last minute," Mr. Grant announced. "A box of chocolates from The Candy Shoppe!"

"Great!" said Brandon. "Finally something I like!"

"Excellent!" said Brooke.

"The perfect birthday gift for Mom!"

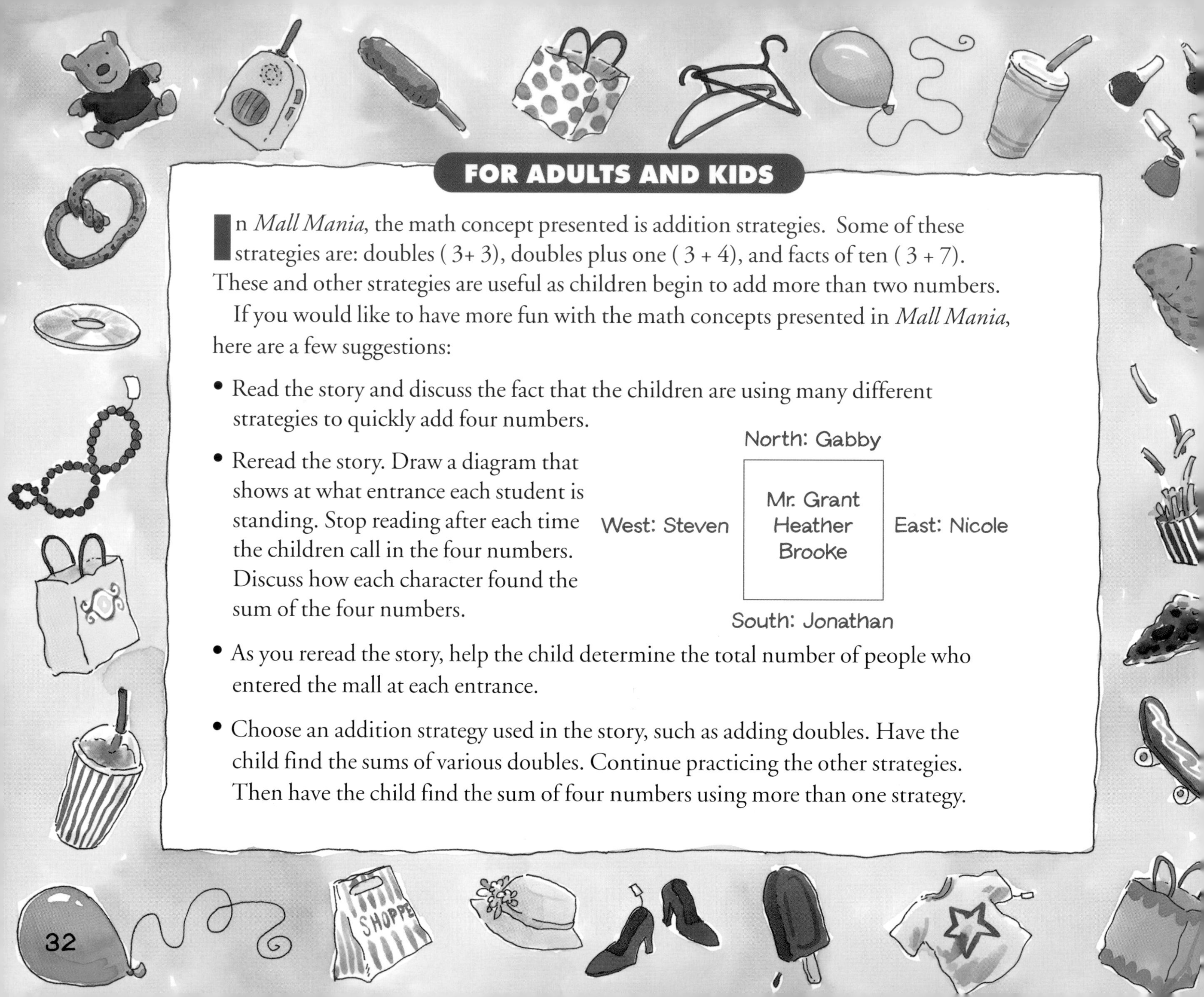

FOR ADULTS AND KIDS

In *Mall Mania*, the math concept presented is addition strategies. Some of these strategies are: doubles (3+ 3), doubles plus one (3 + 4), and facts of ten (3 + 7). These and other strategies are useful as children begin to add more than two numbers.

If you would like to have more fun with the math concepts presented in *Mall Mania*, here are a few suggestions:

- Read the story and discuss the fact that the children are using many different strategies to quickly add four numbers.
- Reread the story. Draw a diagram that shows at what entrance each student is standing. Stop reading after each time the children call in the four numbers. Discuss how each character found the sum of the four numbers.

North: Gabby

West: Steven

Mr. Grant
Heather
Brooke

East: Nicole

South: Jonathan

- As you reread the story, help the child determine the total number of people who entered the mall at each entrance.
- Choose an addition strategy used in the story, such as adding doubles. Have the child find the sums of various doubles. Continue practicing the other strategies. Then have the child find the sum of four numbers using more than one strategy.

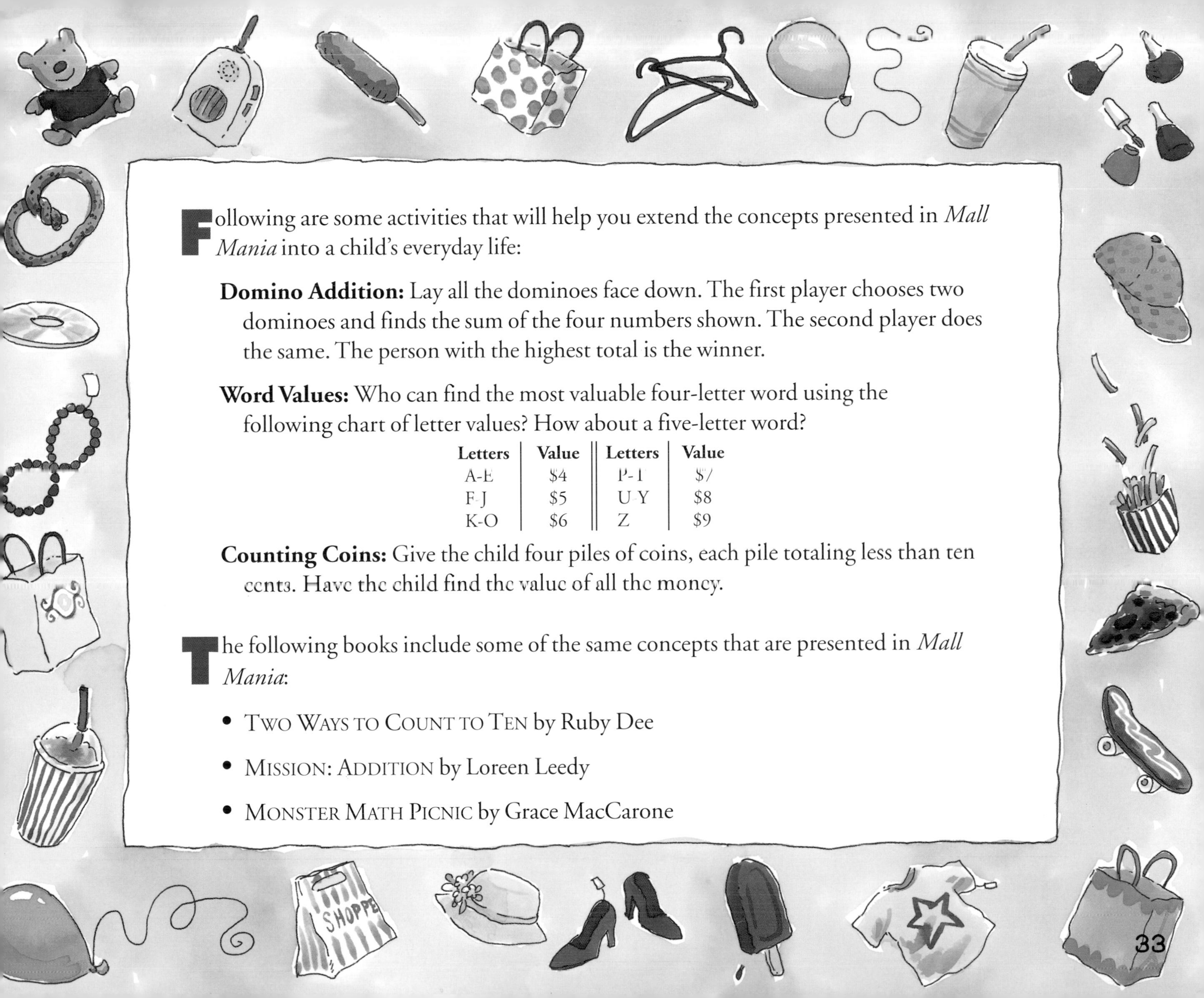

Following are some activities that will help you extend the concepts presented in *Mall Mania* into a child's everyday life:

Domino Addition: Lay all the dominoes face down. The first player chooses two dominoes and finds the sum of the four numbers shown. The second player does the same. The person with the highest total is the winner.

Word Values: Who can find the most valuable four-letter word using the following chart of letter values? How about a five-letter word?

Letters	Value	Letters	Value
A-E	$4	P-T	$7
F-J	$5	U-Y	$8
K-O	$6	Z	$9

Counting Coins: Give the child four piles of coins, each pile totaling less than ten cents. Have the child find the value of all the money.

The following books include some of the same concepts that are presented in *Mall Mania*:

- Two Ways to Count to Ten by Ruby Dee
- Mission: Addition by Loreen Leedy
- Monster Math Picnic by Grace MacCarone

MAY 2006